THE
GAME

–A DARK CORNER NOVELLA –

by

DAVID W. ADAMS

THE GAME – A DARK CORNER NOVELLA

Also available in this series:

The Dark Corner
Return to the Dark Corner
Wealdstone
Resurrection
Wealdstone : Crossroads
Frame of Mind

THE GAME – A DARK CORNER NOVELLA

For Jack & Isabelle,

I know you'll never be able to read this, but you're both the best nephew and niece anyone could ask for.

Love Uncle Dave

x

INTRODUCTION

Welcome to what is the first of hopefully many stand alone stories in the Dark Corner Literary Universe.

I have spent the last three and a half years building up the novels and story collections in the main books, gradually building to an enormous climax with the eighth book, with which I will end the first phase of this universe.

However, whilst doing this, I was plagued by the amount of story ideas swimming around in my brain, and having finished writing Frame of Mind ahead of schedule, and with The Land Beyond not due for release for another four months afterwards, I felt I needed to write something more.

And that's when one of my newfound friends Iona, suggested perhaps taking the same approach one of my favourite authors Christian Francis had taken, and write a novella. Longer than a short story, but smaller than a full length novel, so I could get through the story quickly with no filler. I decided that it was a great idea, and set to work on figuring out the story I wanted to tell.

I knew that I wanted to write something which was from first person as opposed to my usual style of third person, because I wanted to distinguish the novellas from the novels as much as possible. Whilst this story is written in the same universe as all of the other Dark Corner books, I can assure you that it is indeed a stand-alone, one off story not connected to any of the others in any way.

Something people had been asking me for time and time again.

Many of my stories can be read as stand-alones if you want to be technical, but the only one which can really be jumped into without a need for context or background is Resurrection.

Until now, of course.

I have read a lot of horror recently, but then followed it up with a thriller. And then it dawned on me. Not everything in

Wealdstone has to be supernatural. There are some people who are just evil without the need for outside influence.

This is the point where I decided that my story would be from the killer's point of view. But you know me, I like to keep you guessing, and so there are a couple of twists and turns in there, as you would expect from one of my books.

Anyway, enough rambling.

What I will say, is if you have followed my books so far, you will have seen that Frame of Mind was marketed and written as the darkest entry in the series to date.

It's not getting any lighter.

For this reason, I have chosen to once again include content warnings in this book. Please read them, understand the content of the tale before you, and either turn away or proceed with caution.

Thank you for following me on a new part of this journey, and I hope you stay with me for many years to come.

CONTENT WARNINGS

While this story is only a novella, I have managed to cram many disturbing themes and images into these pages, and so please be advised that the story you are about to read contains the following :

- **Blade related injuries**
- **Mutilation**
- **Graphic depictions of violence**
- **Graphic depictions of bodies**
- **Mentions of cannibalism**
- **Sexual Content**
- **Dismemberment**

If any of these themes are triggers for you, please proceed with caution, and take breaks if necessary. Good luck.

ONE

I never intended to kill anyone.

Not the first time anyway.

I know that's easy for me to say at this point, but you must believe me when I say that it was purely a right place, right time situation. Or wrong place, wrong time is what I should have said. You will have to forgive me. I'm not used to trying to explain my inner thoughts. I've spent most of my life being quite private, whether that be in my home, or at work.

I suppose the first time I realised I may have gone too far, was with Jenny. She was certainly the most enjoyable aspect of all the levels I've played in this game of mine. The intimacy and the detail I was able to absorb in such a short space of time was simply… exquisite.

I was almost distracted as I noticed the sun was beginning to set behind the location of the former pier, but my passion kept me going. As I wrapped her small intestine around the preserved 'Welcome to Wealdstone Pier' sign, I paused, but just for a brief moment. I stood back and admired the artwork that I was creating, but something looked a little off to me. The positioning was slightly off centre.

That simply wouldn't do. This game was all about perfection. I demanded it. In all areas of my life, I had always counted on two things. My intelligence, and my attention to detail.

After all what fun is a game without rules?

There is no joy in winning, or no value in losing. Of course, losing the game for me would likely mean losing my life. But the risk? The risk was worth it. The craving I had for something more in my life, to have a purpose, a function, a drive, was simply eating me alive.

I'm so sorry, I realised that you have absolutely no idea what I am talking about. I suppose after that little rant, that you're reaching for a phone and have probably punched in 9-1-1 with your finger hovering over the call button.

Am I right?

Well, before you initiate that movement of your slender digit over the toughened glass of your phone display, and apply the minimal pressure required, allow me to furnish you with a little story. Maybe that way, at least you can begin to understand, or perhaps even sympathise with my plight and how I came to be where I am at this very moment.

But I warn you.

If you think you have heard stories of people slipping into darkness before, think again. This tale will pull you so far into the black emptiness that you may need the help of all the gods simply to climb back to the surface.

Forgive my smile, I can simply feel the creative juices flowing within my mind at the prospect of reliving my work, my craft, once again.

I suppose we should start at the beginning.

TWO

Now the first thing you must understand, is that I have always played the long game. Right back from when I was a child growing up in this dank, skid mark on the underclothes of America.

Pah. America.

What a joke this country has truly become.

Every citizen of this place is so deluded that they are at the pinnacle of greatness, that they cannot see they will be the cause of not only their own doom, but probably that of the entire world. While the so-called fat cats sit on their millions of dollars watching the poor starve to death, and end up on the streets, those who are well-off in their own lives stroll by and pretend nothing matters.

The sympathy and indeed empathy of this country has long gone. Some deluded members of this cavity of humanity cling on to the hope for better things, and that by pulling together everything will rise from the proverbial ashes.

Such nonsense.
Humanity was doomed a long time ago, and America is at the front of the mob lighting the torch.

Anyway, I digress.

The long game.

When I was a small child, I attended Fry Elementary School. It was a fairly respectable institution, sat just within the boundary of Fairmont College to take advantage of a funding loophole which allowed both schools to share funding from two different sources. Clever really. And despicable.

The children there quickly became friends, and groups and cliques formed within the first week. Of course, you must understand, that I was never a part of that. Even at the age of five, I could already tell that I did not fit in with the rest.

Children can be cruel.

I was born with an affliction, passed down from my mother, whereby my left ear was significantly smaller than my right, and my left eye was cobalt blue, whilst my right was a hazel brown.

The bully of the school, not just the year group, was a young man named Roscoe Jenkins.

I know. Such a redneck name.

His appearance matched the name, as did his demeanour. The only reason such a backward child was allowed to dominate the school was because of his substantial size. Not particularly intelligent though. The name he came up for me was simply this.

Wonky.

Not very original, and not technically accurate. It was the latter part of my last sentence which irked me the most. I took pride in my appearance even at such a young age. My polo shirt had its collar pressed and perfectly level. All three buttons were done up tightly to my neck so as to not break the rounded V shape. It was then tucked into my smart khaki trousers in such a way that one small fold of the garment sat neatly on top of my leather belt. The buckle was shined every morning and straightened.

The reason for this was quite simple really. My father. He kept a sharp household. Now by that, I do not mean he beat me or my mother, but his voice was enough to convey importance directly to the recipient of his attention.

If he said that for dinner we would be having meatballs and spaghetti, then that was what we would have. No debate. If he said that the floorboards were squeaking, he would pull them all up and replace them until they were perfectly level and squeak free.

Of course after he had buried our mailman under the living room floorboards, he couldn't exactly replace those, but the rule stuck for the rest of the house.

Hmm? Sorry?

Oh the mailman? Maybe later. Right now, the focus should be on me, after all this is my tale, and we don't have much time now, do we?

Yes, good old Roscoe. He seemed to envy my crisp appearance and how I committed myself to my studies. He would shove me over so I spilled my books everywhere, he would knock my lunch out of my hand and on the rare occasions I had lunch money, he took that too.

On one particular day, he jammed me so hard into my own locker that he dislocated my right shoulder.
That was a trip to the hospital that my parents did not want to make, and so they popped it back in at home. Looking back on it now, I can see their reasoning. At the time, however, I do remember having significant pain in my shoulder for a number of years afterwards.

The second year at Fry Elementary School was my defining year. You see, I had been chosen to join the school band. I had a love for the piano. The accuracy of the notes and pitch within a piece of music, satisfied my precise requirements and brought me genuine pleasure. I recited Moonlight

Sonata in D with such perfection, I was offered the chance to transfer to a school for the gifted near a place called Wellsfield.

My parents, however, maintained that in order to keep a smoothly running household and a family that stayed together, this was quite impossible. I never forgot that. I also never forgot about Roscoe. Or his chums who helped him and laughed at my pain.

Roscoe was my first victim. But it was not at school that I struck the deadly hammer blow. Oh no. As I said to you at the start of this story, I play the long game.
Meticulous planning, and consideration of the consequences and the potential repercussions are vital.

I made my way through elementary school, high school, and even college, all the time being persecuted in the shadow of Roscoe and his pals.

Waiting. Planning. Thinking.

But despite all of this, the execution of this hillbilly reprobate did not come deliberately. At that point, it was all wishful thinking and every time he would flush my head down the toilet after he had used the facility, I would picture him getting hit by a bus, or being arrested.

Until graduation day.

My parents were of course in the audience, as I waited eagerly at the side of the stage for my name to be called up, standing there proud in my gown and hat. Roscoe was stood three students behind me in line, our names being close together alphabetically.

Only Alastair Jarnell now stood before me. As he walked up the stairs, Roscoe thought it would be highly humorous to rip open the back of my gown, and pull down my slacks.

I did not.

As he did so, for the first time in my life, I struck him back. My fist connected with his jaw, and I heard an audible crack and what sounded like a pop from inside his head. His eyes fell upon me, and I watched as his enormous form gradually fell backwards. His body caught the edge of the railings, and he rolled over the top, plummeting down the side of the podium we were standing on.

The caretaker was renovating the grounds at the time, being the end of the academic year, and had propped some of his tools against the side of this podium thinking they would be within close reach. I stood there looking down from above at Roscoe's now impaled and bloated body staring back at me, the prongs of the pitchfork protruding from his torso like Wolverine's claws.

Cerebral edema they called it. Apparently there had been a build up of fluid in the intracellular spaces of his brain. His parents later revealed he had been suffering with nausea and vomiting for a few weeks. Apparently my bop to his head caused it to go pop.

Nobody saw me strike Roscoe. Those standing behind him were part of a tight knit group of friends and were busying themselves with final makeup adjustments, and the crowd were facing the stage at an angle which meant the whole thing had been obscured.

I had killed Roscoe.

And I had gotten away with it.

And I liked it.

THREE

My parents had asked me three times if I saw what happened to Roscoe. I said that I had. I told them that I had watched as his eyes rolled back. That I had watched his body roll over the railings, and that I had seen him impaled on the fork.

I never lied to my parents. Not once.

Truth is the only certainty we have besides death. If you tell the truth, you can never be exposed in a web of deceit. It's just common sense. I believe it was Judge Judy who said once that if you tell the truth, you do not need a good memory.

Much like my father, sometimes, telling the truth came to me at my detriment. You see, he had engaged in an illicit homosexual affair with our mailman. He did not try to hide it. He did not try to shrink away from it. He simply told my mother the same day he completed the indiscretion.

My mother absorbed his confession, and I watched as they bizarrely shook hands, and she left. My mother then returned with the mailman, and led him up the stairs. Moments later, me and my father heard sexual noises upstairs. Despite this, he did not move.

Approximately five minutes later, she descended the stairs, and led my father to the couch, where she told him exactly what she had done. She had slept with the mailman in their bed. My father acknowledged that they had both achieved an equal and therefore balanced status and the matter was closed.

However, despite our perceived weirdness as a family, we were regarded fairly highly within the Wealdstone community. My father was a highly respected dentist, and my mother was a sought after lawyer. The decision seemed so simple to them.

The mailman had to die.

I never actually saw them do it, but I remember hearing three distinct thumps on the floorboards upstairs, and as they returned from the first floor, each carried two trash bags, clearly occupied with some kind of matter. My mother had a small stain on her apron, and my father had red splashes of blood on his wrists and forearm.

They seemed to take no notice of the fact their son was observing all of these details, or that I had already tasted bloodlust, albeit in a mild way. I watched them lift the floorboards in the living room, place the trash bags below them and then carefully replace them, using the same nails as to not arouse suspicion should there be an investigation.

Life continued as normal after that. A year after my graduation from college, I moved into my own apartment near to the beach. It was not a choice I made out of love for the surf, oh my goodness no.

I moved to the beach because I had already decided on my own next target. The long game was now in progress. My targets were very specific, and I knew that I would need to demonstrate the exact level of precision my parents had demonstrated.

You could say that they were my mentors. Not in the way they would have perhaps originally intended, but they certainly impacted my life choices going forwards.

But again, I'm getting ahead of myself.

Let's talk about Andrew.

FOUR

Now Andrew is probably the shortest period of time I have spent completing a level. The levels I speak of, are parts of the game which I must successfully complete in order to move onto the next stage.

One level equals one target, successfully dispatched, and with no comeuppance. Roscoe was the first level. The most basic. The tutorial level if you will. The mailman had been part of the same tutorial, but perhaps with the difficulty increased. Accidental murder an butchery were indeed very different things.

Andrew had been a target for me since elementary school. He was the assistant headmaster of Fry Elementary, and he rose through the schools to the top rank where he became a board member at Fairmont College. I remember him distinctly, even to this day, many years later.

His appearance and style of clothing had never changed in all the years I was aware of him. He was six foot five and a half, so quite a tall fellow and easy to spot in a crowd, though you would rarely find him in one. He was much like myself.

Private. Articulate too.

His renditions of the works of Shakespeare were breathtaking and showed a true love of the craft. However, he was also the one that I brought the attention of my Roscoe problem to. He dismissed the accusation with a very unimaginative line.

"Boys will be boys."

As his mouth uttered those words, flecks of spittle dribbled into his course peppered beard. The flecks of white and grey were present even from his younger years. They were the only aspect of his appearance that did change. More white, less blonde.

When I graduated from Fairmont, I observed him standing to the side of the main stage talking to a young woman from my class. He seemed to be sneering at her, but I couldn't exactly determine what was being said. Then he reached out and stroked

her chest. Her expression changed to one of horror and disgust, and I saw her push him away and walk back towards her friends. He mouthed the word 'bitch' and wandered away himself.
Whilst no detailed assault took place here, the intent of one was very much present. Coupled with his dismissal of my own issues, his name was slid into the game.

Level 2 : Andrew.

Now the idea of this being a game first came about when I played a video game called *Grand Theft Auto V*. The absurdity of the death and mayhem within that game that the main characters got away with struck a nerve within me. My brain is a very logical and methodical one. When things clash with my logic, I must find a way to make them make sense. In my mind, because it was written the way it was, it must have basis in fact.

And so when I moved into my beach-side apartment above the relatively new branch of Footlocker, I began to formulate the game rules.

1. Sufficient time must pass between personal interaction with the level before contact of any kind is made.
2. Do not strike boldly. Make your approach methodical and sensible.
3. Once capture or incapacitation has taken place, at least 72 hours must pass before the level completion is attempted.
4. Only once the level has been completed fully, and no suspicion, rumours or investigation are present, may the next level commence.

These rules had kept me going for almost ten years now, believe it or not. Not once had I violated them, and not once had I failed to complete a level to its entirety.

But back to Andrew.

He had gotten himself into some kind of fracas on the board of Fairmont, attempting to seduce one of the other board members' daughters and so was politely invited to resign, with a neat little payoff. He used the money to but a penthouse apartment in the newest building on the promenade, The Highcliff.

And high it was. Andrew's apartment was on the fifteenth floor, sporting a glass balcony, hot tub, and patio set of the finest rattan material. There's no accounting for taste of course, however much money one has.

I digress.

I had not personally seen Andrew publicly since graduation. I moved into my apartment a year later, and so sufficient time had passed. Rule 1 was attained. Knowing his weakness for vulnerable young women, the next step was to hire the services of a lady that I found on a website known as OnlyFans. I was unaware of this facility, but it has served me well over these years for diversionary tactics and blackmail opportunities. This young woman in particular was not only a content creator, but also escorted on the side for extra cash. Being only twenty-one, she was exactly Andrew's type. I enquired about her availability for 'a friend' from a burner email address. Yes there are burner emails as well as burner phones now. It is the twenty first century, please try to keep up.

She agreed to meet him, the time, place, and services that she would provide, and I paid her in advance by sending cash in an envelope to her PO Box. Most of the workers on the site refused this option, but this lady kindly accepted. Cash is still king apparently, to some people at least.

She understood the assignment and I was not breaking any rules. If anything, I suppose you could say she was a power-up. Andrew thought he had hit the jackpot. I had her behave as though she wasn't really interested to lure him in with his creepy and intimidating ways.

Eventually, giving in and leading him out of the bar I had arranged for them to meet in, one of his regulars just down the street, he took her back to his apartment. Andrew was never one for discretion. Predators in the modern age rarely are. They fucked in front of the glass window of his lounge. Floor to ceiling windows, no curtains. It was an arousing sight, I must say. I sat below on a bench, watching the entire thing, snacking

on a delicious carton of chicken chow mein
from the nearby noodle bar.

I was not illuminated, as the seat I chose was
directly beneath a vandalised street lamp.
Perhaps broken by a drunken youth, or by
one of the seemingly increasing supernatural
occurrences around here. But either way, it
did blur my mind for a moment or two.

You see, I had never known the pleasures of
a woman. It was always discouraged by my
parents. They persevered with the story that
they had only slept together once when I was
conceived, and once on their wedding night.
Besides the mailman 'experiment' they
maintained they observed celibacy. I
suspected that was bullshit.
But watching this beautiful creature
grinding against this grotesque man as her
breasts bounced against the glass of the
window, did begin to stir feelings in me. The
bizarre part was that it wasn't sexual
feelings being aroused.

Showmanship.

If these levels were going to get more and
more complicated, as a game often develops,

then I would need to take greater risks. Andrew certainly was. It was being displayed for all to see after all.

But this was not the time to increase the difficulty once more. This plan was already set in motion. Meticulous and precise.

I finished my food, and placed the container into the nearby trash can, and whilst Andrew was still busy fucking a girl at least half his age, I entered the ground floor of his apartment building. The sign on the door made me smile as I slid through.

'Security system under maintenance.'

I of course, had done my research and discovered the sign was to placate the people living there. No security system had actually been installed. An oversight by the contractors. An oversight that was about to cost Andrew his life.

I rode in the single elevator up and down the floors, remaining alone for twenty minutes. Then, the doors opened on the fifteenth floor. The young woman entered the carriage giving me a brief smile of acknowledgment. She of course did not know who I was, but I knew her. She had not quite successfully reassembled herself following her encounter with Andrew, and her dress was high enough that the bottom of her buttocks were just protruding from beneath the hemline.

As the doors began to close, I lunged forward, seemingly apologetically.

"Oh, I'm so sorry, this is my floor! What a klutz!"

She giggled at me, and waved her hand suggesting it was fine. I had ninety seconds at best between leaving the elevator and the young woman leaving the building, which would then be recorded on the security cameras outside. Not the building ones of course, but those on the opposite side of the street mounted on the lampposts.

I did not wait for the doors to close with the woman inside. I knew that the elevator controls were on this floor. Again, research and planning. Nothing was left to chance here. The level must be completed, it was so early in the game. At the end of the corridor, was Andrew's apartment. Two doors before that was elevator maintenance. I opened the door with a now gloved hand, ensuring no fingerprints were left behind.

No chances taken.

The sound of the cables and the cogs whirring and creaking filled the room. Alongside one of the building generators was a switchboard of fuses and relays. Rather helpfully, the one I needed was marked 'Power : Elevator.'

"Well that certainly is useful."

I spoke aloud, knowing nobody would hear me. Since the building was completed, only Andrew had taken one of the units on this floor. Somewhat of an unnecessary build, really. Much like student accommodation. No students to take the rooms, but let's keep building them anyway!

As I flicked the switch, all the gears and creaking came to a stop, and seconds later, the ring of the emergency help button could be heard on the opposite wall next to a phone. A strange place to put it, given that there were no stairs on this side of the building. And no office for a building superintendent either. Build them fast and build them cheap. Seems to be America's core value.

Again, I digress.

I left the room, closing the door behind me, and made my way to Andrew's apartment. I knocked on the door, making sure to slip my shoes off and shift them to the side. My trousers were long enough to cover my feet to avoid that little curiosity from being discovered. When Andrew opened the door, he was not wearing a shirt or trousers. He had clearly decided to remain in his rainbow coloured boxer shorts for the rest of the night, and was currently sipping from a large glass of whiskey.

"Yeah?"

"Oh hello, Sir. I'm sorry to trouble you this late, but I am the building superintendent, Mr. Stevens."

Andrew looked very confused, but also had an air of disinterest on his face. Almost as if a menial worker was beneath him.
"So?"

His demeanour irked me, but I let it slide. I must keep up my pretence. No chances must be taken.

"There is a young lady in the lobby downstairs who says she may have left her car keys in your apartment. I think she said near your balcony?"

He didn't even question it. The fact the name of the real superintendent was plastered on the lobby walls and on a sign directly opposite the elevator on every floor meant nothing to him. He really did think he was above everyone.

As he turned, he left the door unattended. I slid inside and gently closed the door. There were many weapons dotted around that I could have used, but the plan was the plan. The distraction in the elevator of me lunging for the door with one hand as it closed meant the young woman did not see me grab

the can of mace from her handbag.
Meticulous planning.

I moved across the carpet silently, a reward
for discarding my shoes. As Andrew
approached the now open balcony door, he
knelt forward slightly searching for the
mythical keys. It was only then that he
noticed me behind him.
"Hey, what the fuck?"

The sound of mace spraying is actually a
beautiful moment of ASMR. I suggest you
think about adding it to your list if you enjoy
that sort of thing. His muffled screams of
pain were marred only by the odd expletive.
I didn't need to hear that. I've never been
fond of curse words, although as you have
seen, I do like to throw them out
occasionally.

Logic went out of the window. A normal
person in a normal state of mind, would
consider they were staggering back onto an
open balcony and flailing about. But not
Andrew. Five large steps backwards, and
over the balcony. I didn't hear his screams
as he fell. Whether he was in shock, or
disbelief, I cannot say. I did however, hear

the distant thud as his body impacted the pavement below. I had not set foot near the balcony door, knowing its exposure to those below.

Again, no chances were to be taken.

I slowly exited the apartment, slipped on my shoes, and returned to the control room. I picked up the phone which was now buzzing again, and the young woman's voice came through from the other end.

"Hello?"

"Yeah, hi. The elevator is stuck, and I can't open the doors!"

"Ah, I see. May I ask which floor you are currently stuck on, Miss?"

Being polite is never an effort.

"It's stuck halfway between ten and nine."

I glanced at my watch and set a timer. I could get down to the stairs at the other end of the corridor, and climb down to the ninth floor in less than sixty seconds.

"I am going to activate the emergency power now for you Miss. Once the car begins to move, I need you to press the button for the ninth floor. This is as far as I can guarantee the elevator will reach before the power cuts out. Do you understand?"

A frantic excitement came down the phone.

"Yes of course! I'm happy to take the stairs from there, thank you!"

"Not a problem Miss. Goodbye."
I replaced the receiver and flipped the switch to return power to the car. I left the control room ensuring the door clicked into place. Then the race began. I sprinted down the corridor and into the stairwell. Luckily, I was able to take two steps at a time and I reached the ninth floor in just thirty five seconds, giving me another fifteen to get to the elevator doors.

As they opened, the woman stepped forwards, and bumped right into me.

"Oh my, I'm so sorry Miss! I saw the elevator was out, so I took the stairs, but when I heard the lift moving again, I sprinted to catch it!"

The woman and I scrambled to pick up the contents of her bag which had now scattered over the floor. Including the mace.

"That's okay! The guy told me it's only going this far anyway, so it's the stairs or nothing I'm afraid!"

I began feigning shortness of breath and motioned to a nearby chair sat besides the elevator doors.

"I'll catch my breath a moment first!" I joked.

The young woman giggled and waved goodbye. Just before the doors closed, I darted inside, and hit the button for the ground floor, knowing I would make it out before her. And that I did.

The main entrance was perfectly central to the complex, Andrew's apartment being on the far left, so I was able to leave without anyone noticing. A second timer beeped on my watch as I rounded the corner. Four minutes. Typical response time in Wealdstone for a 9-1-1 call to turn into an on scene response. As if by magic, sirens then wailed and tyres screeched.

I watched from the shadows as two police cars pulled up in front of the entrance, another stopping on the corner, the cops inside visibly shaken at the human pancake before them. As the young woman left the building, she was arrested and immediately placed into custody.

Collateral damage. I could not be seen anywhere near Andrew. Not if I wanted to complete this level.

Rule 2 had been observed. Now for Rule 3. I would not likely be spoken to in relation to this death. I used gloves, there were no cameras present within the building, I used the young lady's mace and made my escape long before she emerged from the building.

The cameras opposite?

Oh don't worry about those. I utilised the blind spot to enter and exit the building. A narrow path along the hedgerow running up to the building.

Seventy-two hours later, the woman was charged with manslaughter. The perception was she had been hired for a night of company with Andrew, but he got a little too keen and she maced him, causing him to fall to his death. She'd likely only serve a year or two given the circumstances.

But she was alive.

And Andrew wasn't.

Rule 3 observed. Onto Rule 4. Level 2 was now complete.

On to Level 3.

FIVE

Now as I said earlier on in this little tete a tete we have been sharing, Andrew's level was the quickest I have ever completed. It was also the simplest. I know a mind as unsophisticated as yours may not be able to comprehend just how simple that second level was for someone with my intelligence, but hopefully by the end of this documentation of events, you shall understand.

Level 3.

Something needed to change. I had previously considered focussing on one task or profession, much as my parents had done. They had been involved in the same line of work from their teen years all the way up to their adulthood and beyond. I didn't want that. I had a distinct plan in my mind that I wished to attain seven doctorates. Yes you heard that right. Seven.

Now to attain those goals, one has to have a blueprint of how your life is going to go.

That brings me to my… shall we say… gaming break.

I fast-tracked myself through a doctorate in engineering within the two years following completion of Level 2. However, it was this doctorate which allowed me to begin Level 3.
Lewis Wilkes.

A man who by all accounts should have been dead a long time ago, without my intervention. I had observed and tracked his movements since my second semester at Fairmont College. I did not know him personally, but he made his name in the local area as a bit of a calamity. He had graduated with honours in the field of Electrical Engineering, but not all of his digits had completed the same journey.

In his very first semester, he managed to slice his left index finger off with a circular saw, and in quite an impressive display, keep the tool running as he swung the other hand in a misguided reaction to his agony, slicing his right pinky finger off in the process.

To this very day I can still see the look of horror in his bulging eyes, the whites almost consuming his pupils, the dark crimson liquid splattering the students either side of him.

Apologies, scenes like that just get my own creative juices riled up. The licking the lips reaction is involuntary, I assure you.

By the time he received his qualifications, he had lost four fingers across both hands, a section of his forearm and three toes. Apparently he was as useless handling hammers and the likes as he was blades.

However, the end results of his work were astounding. He was hired to reconstruct the Wealdstone Pier following the fire there in 2016. It had remained dormant ever since, and the local authority decided to get it renovated and make a big splash in the news with the innovative and grandiose designs.

This was of course delayed following the incidents involving lightning strikes and whatnot. All a bunch of nonsense if you ask me. I was in my apartment during the entire fiasco and I don't remember seeing supernatural beings or creatures of the night or whatever everybody was calling them. Gas mains can do very destructive things when they are ruptured. Ask the people in charge of that god awful shopping district downtown.

Look at me, digressing once again. For someone who likes to keep plans and meticulous records, I do tend to wander off topic.

Anyway, the plans were put forward when they started the rebuild of the main street area. Lewis who had been vacationing with his parents in Trinity Bay at the time, returned with a team of just a few contractors he trusted, determined he could get the whole thing built and operational in four months. The mayor guffawed at the suggestion until he realised the potential news headlines that could prove quite lucrative. He was always looking to boost his reputation, or bank balance and had been receiving under the counter encouragement for over twenty years.

That is a long time for a parasite to go unopposed. Imagine if Donald Trump had been our President for more than the four years he was in office. I don't often shudder but that one always sends a chill down my spine.

Sorry what was that? Lewis?

Oh dear reader, you thought that Lewis was my target? Oh my, no. The Mayor was my target.

Lewis was simply a means to an end.

The long game has always involved long and stringent planning, and I needed to know where and when he would be most vulnerable, and Lewis provided those details in a local bar called Sisko's the night before construction was due to start.
Never could hold his drink. Something he and my mother had in common, not that my father ever knew. Being a lawyer in America was about as soulless as one could get, so she would drink away her day in her office, and then down three pots of coffee before leaving to sober her up. Very clever. He never knew, but I noticed the changes in behaviour during the week from her leaving to returning home. The careless placing of an

empty miniature gin bottle in the recycling didn't exactly help.

"So I got paid shit tons, man. Like the job is only gonna cost half of what the mayor is payin' me. Told me to keep the rest if I get it done ahead of schedule."

"Interesting," I remarked. "Surely that would mean cutting down on materials?"

I was certainly feeling more like an investigative reporter. I was also taking quite a chance in chatting in the open like this in the most popular bar in Wealdstone. But such is the nature of the game.

Each level must be progressively harder, and as I am the only one who knows I am playing such a game, I must make things harder for myself to make the reward of completing a level so much sweeter.
"Oh yeah. He got six million for the project from funding. I get a million of that, a million for the cheaper materials and he gets the rest. A million bucks. Can you imagine what I can do with that?"

Acquiring a brain transplant or prosthetic digits came to my mind immediately, but I simply bought him another drink and allowed his rambling to continue.

"He's insisted on buying the stuff himself though. Wants to be hands on so he can take more credit. Fine by me, I hate the limelight."
Vital information.

"And how long will it take him to complete such a transaction?" I asked tentatively.

"Not long buddy. He's meeting the suppliers on the pier this Friday at 9. Hoping to start building next week. A delay from starting tomorrow as planned, but hey whatever saves some dollars right?"

Articulately put. Time frame now in place, I could engage the final part of my plan. The execution of the level. This one would be more intricate than Andrew's level. It would involve direct action from myself in his execution.
You are probably thinking at this point, that I'm not all that bad. The mayor is taking bribes so therefore he is one of the bad guys.

And Andrew was a bit of a predator, so no harm, no foul. I appreciate the sentiment, dear reader, but I'm afraid I must correct you there. My targets for each level have been chosen for at least three years before I take them out. The execution of the plan however can take any amount of time.

I'll explain how they are chosen a bit later on in these pages. Also, I do hope you appreciate how I chose black pages to document these details. I suspected I may be called into an act of self-preservation during these recollections, and black ink would not show up the blood should there be any, and ruin my words. Just a little consideration from me to you.

Now, the amount of time that passed between my conversation with Lewis and the proposed meeting between the Mayor and the contractors was just enough time to ensure I was not spotted recently with Lewis and therefore would limit my connection to him, despite the public nature of said chatter. I made my way onto the pier two hours in advance. I have always been an excellent swimmer, and the tattered end of the pier resembled a ladder, so scaling it was not too difficult. The added absence of any lighting that far out was also advantageous.

They were late. That was the first thing to piss me off. Oh there I go again with the swearing. Apologies, but when I go to such lengths to ensure punctuality and have everything prepared, I do not appreciate tardiness. There was also another problem.

The Mayor was not alone. He brought his son with him. This would complicate things. I could feel my blood beginning to boil and the prospect of failing the game at just the third level was infuriating. I had to try and keep my emotions in check, because I was raring to launch at them both with my bowie knife, and despite my effective skills, I would still be outgunned so-to-speak if they both defended themselves.

I watched silently from the shadows as the transaction was completed, and the contractors left. It was very nineties cop show orientated. The nodding of heads, passing of the briefcases, shaking of the hands, and then the usual choice of one party to wait until the other is out of sight before choosing to leave themselves. In this case, it was the Mayor and his boy who decided to stay.

I moved my way towards them, again skulking in the shadows, knife clutched in my right fist leaving my left hand free to grab the head of this bloated ignoramus. The difficulty level increased however, when my foot caught a discarded beer can, no doubt from some drunken idiot trying to fumble with his date at some point.

"What was that?" asked the son.

"No idea, go check it out."

How nice of the Mayor to send his only son into the darkness and risk his safety rather than check himself. Whilst the plans were now almost totally out of the window, this separation did return to me somewhat of an advantage.

The son made his way towards me, but his eyes were not fully adjusted to the increased darkness the further back he went on the pier, and so as he completely walked past me, I snuck in the other direction towards his old man. Once again, I removed my shoes, and slid them up against a piece of the iron railings that were still intact, making a mental note of where they were. I moved across the wooden surface like a panther. No sound at all.

As I brought myself up to full height behind him, I placed my cool hand on his forehead, and gripped it tightly.

"Wh…?"

Before he could get an entire word out, I flashed the thick blade against his throat. One clean cut from ear to ear, curving below his Adam's apple, finishing with a flourish. The construction of the blade was so exquisite that I actual felt the vibration of the sinews and tendons spring apart against the metal. The sensation was very pleasing.

There I go again, licking my lips.

I allowed the Mayor to slip to the floor carefully, which was no mean feat given his much larger size in comparison to myself. But although I believed the level to be on the verge of completion, I was not at all prepared for what happened next.

"Hey! Who the fuck are you!"

The voice came from behind me, and
pierced my ears like an arrow. An instant
shiver shot up through my body, and my
blood ran cold. The son was now standing
somewhere behind me.

I cannot explain what happened next as
anything other than instinctive reaction. I
span on the spot, and launched the huge
bowie knife through the air. Given the
darkness, he did not see the flash of
moonlight against the metal blade until it
was too late. The tip pierced his chest with
an audible thud, and if I'm not mistaken, the
sound of scraping bone as it embedded itself
within his torso.

The fear of being caught had blurred my
senses, and I could no longer see a clear
image of the son. It was only a few moments
later when my heart had stopped thundering
in my ears that I heard the gargled sound of
the boy coughing up his own blood, followed
by the bigger relieving sound of his body
hitting the floor.

A strange feeling then shot through me. The
son had apparently fallen forwards, and
when the handle of the still protruding knife

hit the deck, it pushed itself further into him, until I saw the tip of the blade protruding from his back glinting in the moonlight.

I had a shiver of what at the time I could not explain, run through my entire body. I later realised it had been… pleasure. The sound of the metal slicing flesh was like an injection of endorphins directly into my brain. I vaguely remember an audible squeak of joy.

This feeling was short lived however, when I actually mustered enough courage to examine the scene properly. The son had kicked my shoes over the edge of the pier during his approach. The second issue, was that his Apple Watch was now lighting up with an incoming call. Somebody knew he was out, and they would soon be looking for him.

My perfect plans ruined. The studies of engineering now pointless as the initial plan of having the pier collapse was no longer viable. My clothing was tied to this place, and now it was gone. Perhaps it would wash up on the beach, or wash up in Argentina. It didn't matter. The simple fact was that now something was out of my control.

My skin began to itch and my body began to convulse. It was almost as if the rush of pleasure was a drug and this was the melancholy to follow withdrawal.

Level 3 was at risk of failure. And I had to fix it.

Somehow.

SIX

Everything was collapsing in my mind. My measurements now meant nothing. My plans were destroyed. I would surely fail this level, and in spectacular fashion.

Or at least that is what I thought.

I don't recall how I returned home, how long it took, or any of the journey whatsoever. I remember waking up on the floor of my living room the next morning, and glancing up at the clock to see it was eleven-thirty-five. I quickly reached for the TV remote and flicked to the news channel.

Nothing.

No reports of the death of the mayor or his boy. No mention of shoes being washed ashore. Everything was exactly as it should have been.

And then I saw them.

My shoes were on the doormat, perfectly shined, polished and looking at me. I zoned out for what felt like an eternity, before it dawned on me. Somebody must be in my apartment.

I kept an array of blades around my home just in case of a situation like this. I called them my 'inventory' and as I reached under the coffee table, I felt for the dagger that was usually there.

Gone.

Now my skin was on fire with anxiety, and my forehead dripped sweat into my eyes. The stinging was a mere inconvenience and I darted towards the bookcase on the far wall, opening up a hollow volume from the second shelf.

Empty.

"What the fuck is going on?"

I figured if ever I was going to embrace the curse words, now was the time. Somebody unknown to me had brought me home somehow, retrieved and cleaned my shoes, and removed the weapons from my apartment. But despite all of this, I never heard any breathing, or footsteps or noises

of any kind. I had one more knife that I kept
hidden in another book.

This book was not a hollowed out volume,
but a rather poignant poetry collection that I
adored. The blade in question could be
mistaken for a novelty bookmark. Of course
it wasn't. As I moved over to the end table
by the couch and picked up by copy of
Ouroboros Thoughts, I saw the blade was
still there marking a page as if it was indeed
a bookmark.

I slipped it out, gently placing the book back
on the mahogany wood surface. I stalked my
way around the living area, and into the
kitchen. Each step was like a venture into
the unknown. Everything had been perfect.
Calculated.
Measured. Neat.

Until last night.

The apartment was clear. There were no
intruders. Whoever had brought me home
and removed my weapons had left no trace.

Except one.

As I slumped back on the couch, trying to gather my thoughts and strike the panic from my chest, the letterbox rattled and an envelope shot through the door. I didn't get mail. Ever. I paid all utility bills online, and subscribed to nothing.

I slowly walked over to the mat which now contained my shoes and the letter. It had no address on the front. Just a name. Mine.

Armand Jellico.

I am aware I had not previously shared my name with you, but of course you already knew that. I have somewhat of a reputation by this point. No, my parents were not French, nor were they fans of *Star Trek*. My name was merely a happy sounding noise to the people who raised me. They were fans of almond nuts and jelly on sandwiches. Not exactly a legacy kind of name, but without the context, I feel it sounds rather sophisticated.

Armand.

Sounds like a *Pink Panther* villain. Perhaps a jewel thief. But whoever wrote this letter knew who I was, and I suspected not for tax reasons. I wrenched my front door open, and looked quickly down either side of the corridor. But the person had already fled. Returning to the apartment and closing the door, I picked up the letter, and noticed my name was written not in black ink... but dried blood.

I turned over the envelope, and the back was not sealed with saliva applied to the sticky strip, but simply tucked into the base of the envelope. I lifted the tab outwards, and extracted the crisp white paper, unfolding it. I have the note here, and so I shall read it to you word for word.

"Armand,

Games never truly begin to excite until you reach the higher levels. I was growing weary of your laboured approach... this so called long game. I decided to advance you past 'GO'.
Your $200 however, comes in the form of this gift...

Level 3 is complete."

I was unsure what came over me, but I slid the letter back into the envelope, and sealed it exactly as it had been delivered to me, and I felt an immense smile spread across my face. The panic of the morning and previous night were gone. The endorphins were swimming in my mind, and had I been a dancing sort of chap, I would have leapt in the air or done a jig. I now knew that the dried blood on the letter belonged to the Mayor, or perhaps his son. But I knew something far more intriguing.

This was now a two player game.

SEVEN

I am not a stupid man by any means. I do not let excitement get the better of me. And it was for this reason, that I decided to continue the long game approach I had become accustomed to, but rather than progress with Level 4, the long game I refer to was the waiting game. Part of me was eager to continue but I was too curious to see what would happen if this mysterious second player got fed up of waiting.

I continued my studies that I mentioned earlier, and achieved my doctorates in chemistry and entomology. This was obviously not a six week process. Two years had passed since Level 3 had indeed been completed by whoever this mystery player was.

The Mayor's death did not come into the news for several weeks after I killed him. His son's still hasn't, even to this day. Luckily another proposed supernatural occurrence happened around the same time involving a cult on the edge of town somewhere, and the Mayor was attributed to joining that group and meeting a sticky end as a result.

I was impressed by that turn of events. Because of the circumstances surrounding this cult, everything was handled delicately and brushed under the rug. Not exactly the news headlines he had been hoping for when he was alive, but he did indeed make the front pages.

The pier ended up being demolished rather than renovated, and the waterfront is slated for development in the next eighteen months.

Nobody knows what happened to Lewis. CCTV caught him getting on to a train a week after the Mayor's body was found, and nobody has seen him since.

Player Two, however, did make another appearance. Again, it was in the form of a letter posted through my door.

"Armand,

I told you the long game was tiresome. I'm stood at the proverbial arcade machine. I have placed my quarter into the coin slot. The screen is now reading 'waiting for player 2'.

Won't you join me?"

Eagerness consumed me and I felt butterflies in my stomach. But in all honesty I wasn't sure where to go from here. I had been shown that my multiple rules, plans, and precision counted for nothing. Everything went to hell that night, and I still got away with it. The intervention was welcome, but I was still breathing and not in a jail cell.

It excited me.

The recklessness. The abandonment. The risk. I had undervalued the rewards of being so careless and escaping punishment and retribution. However, it was clear that Player Two was waiting for me to make my move. I suspected the competition before me would involve inventiveness. This was something that could be planned. But I decided not to do so on this occasion. Introducing another player was exciting, but the levels still needed to become harder, as is the nature of a true game.

And that is where the previously mentioned Jenny entered the frame. Now take a deep breath, because this is where you may think you're hearing a different person talk.

Let's talk about how I fell in love.

EIGHT

I had wandered along the promenade for an hour or so, contemplating the possible targets for Level 4. A few names came to mind. Drug dealers who had escaped punishment. A fairly young chap who worked in the soup kitchen on Franklin Street who always seemed to be unimpressed with anything. I even considered trying to track down Player Two themselves.

And then I saw her.

The coffee stand opposite the former location of the pier was usually empty. The prices were exceptionally high and after the recent problems in the town, people just didn't have the money. Nine dollars for a cup of dark caffeinated liquid was rather excessive. But this day, there was a line of twenty people. It did not take me long to see why.

A stunningly beautiful woman was serving the drinks. Long wavy hair, a mixture of blonde and dark brown which hung to her shoulders. Her skin was tanned evenly and perfectly. Her left strap of her top slid down as she knelt to get more cups. No tan lines. Her face was fixed in a perma-smile and her teeth were uniform and perfect, shining a true pearl white in the sun. Her tight tank top was most likely the cause for the twenty men waiting for a coffee. Black, cut in a plunging v-neck exposing the line of her ample cleavage. And two noticeable thin lines almost central to her breasts.

Piercings.

I never did understand why people did that. But it did allow the muscled perverts the knowledge that she was not wearing a bra. Her smile was painted on for the good of her business, and every so often, she would lean forwards deliberately and suddenly the man at the front of the queue would buy a flapjack or a muffin. More dollars in the jar I suppose.

I joined the back of the queue and watched with interest. Her motions were almost identical for each customer. A smile, enquiry as to their wellbeing, and then the question of what they would like. More often than not, the response would be 'your number' or something similar. She would squeeze her cleavage together, or bend over and the sale would increase, and then the person would leave, and it would start all over again. Eventually, it was my turn to head up the line, which had now dissipated, given the late hour of the day.

"Hey there! How are you doing this fine evening?"

Her voice was slightly harsher than it had sounded from the back of the line. A voice of experience. Not all of it good. I absorbed more details about this woman. The stance she took behind the bar, the way she flicked her hair over one ear but never the other.

"I am quite well thank you…"

I held out for her name. Another detail that I needed to have.

"Jenny. And yours?"

Time to be reckless and throw away the rules.

"Armand. Nice to meet you."

She smiled at my name, tinted with a quizzical flash of curiosity in her eyes.

"And you… Armand. What can I get for you?"

"Oh, I'm not actually sure. I was curious about why the quietest stand on the sea front was suddenly the busiest. It was niggling at me."

I gave her the most genuine smile that I could, and she shied away slightly, and a smaller smile crept her way across her mouth.

"And did you manage to figure that out?" she asked cheekily.

I returned the smile.

"I think I've worked it out, yeah."

She giggled and swept her hands across the bar as a nervous reflex.

"Well, may I suggest the cherry iced latte? It's our special today and is perfect for these… hot nights."

I'd briefly looked away but when I looked back, I thought I caught the tail end of her winking at me.

"Sounds good, I'll take one."

I tapped my credit card on the contactless reader, and she turned to prepare the drink. I had never before been infatuated with anyone, attracted to anyone, or had any interest in a relationship either romantic or casual. It was far too unpredictable and not easy to plan around. And so I avoided it.

But this woman… there was something about her. I *wanted* her. I cannot explain it even to this day. Some unknown desire was consuming me, and no amount of iced cherry latte was going to cool me down.

We chatted for what seemed like an hour but was actually nearer to two. She told me all about her brother who was in the Marines, and her younger sister who had been in prison for the last few years. The coffee stand was her first job in a long time. While she was beautiful without question to anyone with eyes, she didn't see it. Despite everything provided as evidence, she was insecure about her appearance. An issue I put to one side later that night.

She was ten years younger than myself, and it showed. As we undressed each other back at my apartment, her skin was a joy to caress. Smooth, unblemished, a true work of art. The piercings in her nipples glinted in the dim light of the lamp, and her kisses felt like a soft cushion of air upon each touch to my own. Her backside was exquisite, and as her breasts moved in front of my face as she rode my hips on the couch, I made mental notes of every single inch of this woman. Birthmark on her left buttock, slightly off centre. The deep and hypnotic forest green of her eyes. The way the beads of sweat slid down the small of her back. Every detail stored in my mind, creating a picture perfect image of this naked goddess.

As I said, she truly was a work of art. I was in love. Now I know what you must be thinking. How can a killer fall in love? Nobody's first time is ever that good, especially once they've hit forty.

You misunderstand me. I did not fall in love with Jenny. I fell in love with the fact that

Jenny was *a work of art.* You see you have to listen carefully.

The sex was amazing, whether you choose to believe that or not. Between that first time and the morning, we visited every room in my apartment and the shower afterwards. At precisely nine-fifteen that next morning, she kissed me softly on the lips, and strolled out of my apartment door.

And I knew what I wanted to do next.

NINE

I had not spoken to my parents in over five years, but the day after my encounter with Jenny, my father knocked on my door. They knew where I lived, they made no attempt to contact me, and this came completely out of the blue. Clearly it was not just me that was beginning to abandon the planning and measured approach.

I opened the front door after the distinct three knocks echoed around my living room, and there he stood. The man I had always admired as a neat and presentable creature was now scruffy, dishevelled and sporting a pained expression on his face. He said no words, but simply looked at me. I stepped aside and allowed him to stumble into the apartment, closing the door slowly behind him as I tried to absorb the image now presented to me.

"Your mother."

This was the only verbal communication I received from my father before he closed his eyes and slumped on my sofa. He was not dead, but clearly exhausted from whatever trauma he had experienced. I knew immediately she was dead. What I did not know was how. And perhaps at whose hand.

I was reluctant to leave him in my apartment as I had replenished my weapons and supplies, and plans were underway for the much anticipated Level 4, which I was now eager to begin. However, this was important. I needed to see what had happened to the woman who had raised me. I needed to see the state that had created this unknown version of my father. And so I left. I do not own my own vehicle, and so I took the keys from my father's jacket and saw his cherry red Crown Victoria parked askew in my parking space. The irony in a killer now driving an ex police vehicle was not lost on me, and in fact made me smile slightly. I remember the day he picked it up from the police auction and took it for a respray. It was a mere fortnight after they had dispatched the mailman, and I remember thinking about how audacious it was to even attend a police auction, let alone purchase something.

The drive to my old home was longer than I remembered. Perhaps it was due to the fact I was thinking of Jenny. The birthmark, the smile, the hair, the smooth perfect skin. Art.

When the house loomed into view, it was in a similar condition to the man I had just left back at my complex. Weeds and shrubs had grown through the pathways, the hedgerow had sprouted outwards and collapsed the previously white picket fence onto the now cracked driveway. With nowhere else to leave the car, I drove over the panels, each one cracking and fracturing under the tyres. Clambering out, the stench hit me immediately in the summer air. Flesh. And not the fresh variety. Something told me that the events leading up to my father's knock at my door were actually older than I was led to believe.

The front door was slightly ajar, not from being left that way, but from vines of ivy having crept over the doorstep and into the house itself. Had this house not been relatively isolated at the far end of the street, I suspect neighbours would have been calling the police in their droves, with the smell so attainable outside of the house.

The entrance hall was actually not too dissimilar to the condition I remembered. Leaves were strewn across the old wooden floor but the house itself was not in too bad a condition. There was, however, no need to search around the house to find the source of the smell.

My mother's body was on display on the dining room table. And when I say on display, I mean *on display*.

Her head had been hacked across the throat, but not all the way through, and so it hung back over the edge of the table. Her arms were splayed open, each side of the wound pinned back with galvanised nails into the surface of the wood itself.

Her legs were in similar condition, the only difference being that her feet had been removed at the base of the shin, and placed between her legs, pointing towards the bottom of the table, much in the same way my shoes had been left for me.

The always tightly buttoned blouse my mother wore had been neatly cut open, but not removed. Either side had been pulled to the side, the buttons missing, in order to expose my mother's chest. The chest in question was the most intricate display I had ever seen in my life either at my own hand or in any movie I had ever bore witness to.

A single incision had been made perfectly central from the base of her neck wound all the way down to her navel. A cross section ran from beneath her left breast directly parallel, ending beneath her right breast. Again, the skin had been pulled back at points, and pinned using galvanised nails, this time of a much longer size to enable the object to pass through the rest of the body and through the table.

Her ribs had been cut with such neatness and skill, each one then removed, and turned vertically creating a void in the centre, which now displayed all of my dead mother's organs. The organs themselves were untouched, simply available for all the world to see.

As I moved around the table to look at my mother's face, I noticed that her mouth was agape, and her eyes were wide, suggesting at least some of this brutal act was done while she was still alive. Her eyes themselves, however, had been replaced. In their place were now two buttons from the aforementioned blouse, a single trickle of blood trailing just beneath them.

After a few moments of examination, I stood at the base of this display and simply stared. The level of decomposition would suggest at least a week had gone by since this was orchestrated. The question now was who was responsible. My father? No. The condition he was in told me everything I needed to know.

But the feet. It was the feet.

A small smile began to spread across my face as I realised the perpetrator behind this crime. My mother had been killed and put on display by Player Two. My eyes wandered once more over each intricate detail of the arrangement. The cuts, the angling of the ribs, the position of the feet, the placing of the button in the eye socket. A new appreciation washed over me, a desire to do better, and to improve my own craft. The woman on the table may have been my mother, but the desire within me to emulate this level of skill burned in my chest like a raging fire, and any emotional attachment was now buried in the embers of that fire. If there was any lingering doubt to the person behind this creation, that was soon gone upon my return to my apartment, and the equally violent condition of my father.

TEN

Burying my parents was not something I had enjoyed. To a normal person, it would have been due to high levels of emotion, regret at things unsaid, the loss of a oved one. For me however, it was the sheer workload that came with it. I had taken the decision to utilise my new tools and supplies to first dismember them both. This was made easier by the condition of the bodies that Player Two had left them in. The head required very little effort to remove, the feet were already separated, and although a little inventiveness was required, I soon had both bodies ready to move.

The workload was the disposal. My mother's body was not too difficult, I simply raised the living room floorboards, and placed her remains alongside the mailman before replacing them. I was amazed at the quality of the trash bags they had used in his concealment. Even now, no stench leaked out and no evidence of bodily fluids or decomposed flesh were remotely evident. Fortunately for me, they still had some of that brand in the kitchen for me to utilise myself. My father's body on the other hand, required moving out of the building before being transported. That was more difficult. The complex I lived in had varied over the last few years. As I said, when I moved in, the unit below was a newly opened branch of Footlocker, but after the countless events in Wealdstone, the larger brands were pulling out quickly, and so the unit was converted into an extension of the upstairs and the whole building was now an apartment complex.

Which meant other neighbours.

Nosy neighbours.

I decided it was much more appropriate to enlist some help. And so I played a reckless card. One which excited me even more. I decided to call Jenny. She was more than happy to help, and excited to see me again. She told me how she couldn't stop thinking of our night together, which I took as a huge compliment, and she was on a day off from the coffee stall and rushed over to join me. Naturally, I did not tell her what was in the bags, I simply told her I was disposing of some old paperwork from the office. That office in question was how I made my living. I worked as private detective for two years to help hone my skills in avoiding detection, planning and the likes.

When I ceased that line of work, I sub-let the office to a pet grooming company who paid me rent, which paid my bills and also allowed my free time to be utilised towards the game.

The game. A new dimension to Level 4 had arisen. No longer was this level about me taking down my next target and getting away with it, but now it was the disposal of the two bodies lain before me by Player Two. And to increase the difficulty, Jenny would help me do so.

"These bags are so heavy," she said as she placed the third trash bag into the new garbage chute.

"Yeah, well reams of paper are heavy," I retorted.

I saw her try and pick one bag up by the bottom, and her hand retracted quickly. I suspected these bags were not as impressive as I initially thought.

"It feels slimy inside this bag."

I made an effort to laugh this away quickly.

"Yeah, I may or may not have knocked over an entire coffee pot into some of these boxes. Apparently coffee and paper don't mix well."

It worked, and Jenny laughed it off. Once every bag was loaded into the chute, we dusted off our hands and returned to the apartment. The sex this time was even better than the first. Jenny had decided she needed a shower from all of the manual labour and invited me to join her. The initial annoyance of this location not being particularly ideal or suitable given how small and slippery it was, was soon dispelled by the sensations created by Jenny and her movements.

We spent an hour afterwards just lying naked on my bed, talking about how she didn't feel at home in Wealdstone, and she was a little scared by how often the town seemed to be making the news for one reason or another. I understood her concerns, but my mind was still focussed on completing the newly reorganised Level 4. My father's body parts were still sat at the bottom of the garbage chute and would need removing as soon as possible. I chose the chute because this would place the bags at the rear of the building which is not overlooked by any other buildings or cameras. This would allow me to load them into the car and drive them away.

Jenny planned to leave the following week. She had made her mind up, and she had no intention of continuing our little meet-ups. She therefore decided to spend as much time together as possible before she left. This posed a problem for me, because I had received another note from Player Two posted through my door the night before. It would appear they had gotten fed up of waiting. The note read as follows.

'Armand,

I attempted to entice you along by completing half of the next level for you, but I suppose I did not do enough. Level 4 remains uncompleted, and I am growing weary. I fear

*if you do not move on to Level 5 soon, I will
have no choice but to complete the game with
you."*

I had read the note twice, and it was not a
typo. 'Complete the game *with* you.'

For the first time, I was concerned for my
own safety. I had considered that me and my
unknown colleague were just that. Joint
players in the game, each competing against
the other. Now it became clear. The
competition was not friendly, and this was
now a fight to the death.

I walked to the kitchen to get myself a glass
of water, and when I came back, Jenny had
fallen asleep on the bed. The sun shone
through the gaps in the blinds, illuminating
her skin perfectly. But what I didn't see was
a woman I desired. A woman I loved with all
of my being. No. What I saw was a series of
dotted lines all over her body. An outline
tracing itself down her back where the spine
could be extracted.

Another line moving in a curved shape
where her lips could be removed. Circular
shapes where her nipples including piercings

could be cut away for display purposes. The possibilities were endless. The desire was rampant, but not for her company. For her... parts.

Not tonight, however, I thought. Tonight I would rest. I required every ounce of mental acuity to complete Level 4 successfully before even considering Level 5. I felt that time was running out.

And all the time, my father's dismembered corpse was rotting at the bottom of the garbage chute.

ELEVEN

The next morning, I awoke at five-fifteen. Jenny was long gone, having woken up just after midnight and feeling uncomfortable staying over when she had so much packing to do. We had enjoyed another brief round of intercourse before I wished her well, and saw her out the door. I snapped into sleep almost immediately and awoke to the sound of my alarm radio. Old school, as the young people call it, but I found it more efficient than a bell or a phone vibrating.

It would be another hour until the sun came around to this side of the building, and so I dressed, applied no cologne as to not create a distinguishing smell around the corpse or the area in which to dispose it, and then left. My father's car had been parked downstairs on and off for four days now. A neighbour had already commented on how it was about time I decided to drive more. I seriously considered her as a contender for Level 5, but I did not have time to dwell on it.

I sauntered down the stairs, my plan clear in my mind. I made my way to the car, and drove it around to the back of the complex, close enough to not have to carry the bags far, but not so close as to warrant suspicion. But that was, as it turns out, the least of my problems.

The garbage bay was empty.

I stood motionless for a moment or two, before diving forward and examining the area in close detail. No. It was true. All of the garbage was gone. I felt the rush of panic burning within me and once more my skin prickled and began to itch. How was this possible? The garbage men don't come for another two days. Where was my father's body, and who could have done this?

Player Two. It had to be. But I had no way of getting in touch with them, and that was when I realised that this was out of my hands. There was absolutely no way of tracking them down. The cameras in our building never worked, and even when they were, they were positioned to avoid the stairwell, and none of them watched over the front doors of the apartments. The excuse the neighbourhood watch came up with was that it was to ensure the privacy of residents.

That was of course an ignorance that I had enjoyed up until now. Now, it was a hinderance to a problem I did not have a solution to.

I sat in my apartment for the next four hours, contemplating what to do. But four hours was all I was given. There was a knock at the door, and I sprang to life, rushing to open it. Standing there was my mailman. I had seen him in the building before, but as I never got mail, I had never interacted with him. My mind flashed back to my parents and their encounter with the mailman before his demise. I considered it, if only to find some contorted comfort in a childhood memory. I decided he wasn't physically attractive enough to indulge myself, and I was certainly in no mood to dispatch another body. I took the package he presented to me, nodded my thanks, and closed the door.

The parcel was wrapped in plain brown paper, and tied neatly with a string. The address label informed me this was a package which was overnight mailed, sent out at one o'clock that very morning. A highly efficient service indeed, I thought to myself. Until I opened it.

The smell hit me first, the heat second. Inside the box was a coil of human intestine, tightly wrapped. But the intestine had been *cooked*. The inside of the box was lined with silver insulation, which had clearly preserved the heat, and behind that insulation, poking out, was a white envelope. I closed the box having removed the envelope, and examined it. I already knew who it was from. I opened it, and read the note aloud to myself.

'Armand,

I saw that you were dawdling along with that pretty little coffee shop girl of yours, and I decided to help you out slightly. You cannot complete Level 4, let alone jump to Level 5.

Once again, I have lent you a hand. But no more. I took care of your father for you. It was an interesting experience examining your family home. I placed his remains carefully alongside your mother, and of course the mailman.

You can now consider the level complete in our little game. However, I decided to get a head start on you for Level 5.

I hope you like the pretty gift I sent you. Jenny wasn't a fan when I suggested it, but it was quite hard to decipher some of her words as I sliced open her smooth, soft belly. A mental note for next time I suppose, would be to bring a gag when I choose to disembowel people while they're alive. Still, her intestines cooked nicely in the heat from the house fire. Oh yes, I suspect the police will want to talk to you when they examine the wreckage. Just a little heads-up.

My Level 5 has begun, and yours is about to come to an end.'

Jenny. He had killed Jenny.

But worse than that, he had burned down my family home, with the butchered remains of three people inside. I took from his suggestion that the fire was not the result of accelerant and therefore would not cremate the bones. He wanted me to be in the frame for this. He knew now that my entire family was dead, that I would be the logical prime suspect. And he had taken Jenny.

I had to get rid of her intestines. This was as incriminating a piece of evidence as was possible to have. And then it hit me. I had done nothing to Jenny's body. All of the injuries were caused by Player Two. If I didn't handle these body parts bare handed, and kept them inside the box, there would be no evidence tying me to her death.

My parents were another problem, but Jenny was here. Now. I decided to try and get my own Level 5 up and running. But this was not a level to complete the execution of a target. No. The game had changed.

Now, the game was who would get caught first.

TWELVE

I did have a slight pang of regret at the
action I was now taking, but I quickly
reminded myself that it was not I who had
altered the game. I was quite happy playing
along as I began. One person for each level,
gradually increasing the difficulty. But no.
Player Two had changed the rules. Changed
the objective. And here I was, trailing
Jenny's intestines around the 'Welcome to
Wealdstone Pier' sign which remained
despite the structure's demolition, as a piece
of historical significance. A slight adjustment
was required to make sure it hung centrally.
I had used one fo my new blades to slice the
intestine down the middle in order to widen
the surface area slightly.

If you know your anatomy, then you will
know the true length of the lower intestine,
so you can imagine the splendour that now
greeted me after an hour of hard work. After
the fire at the house had made the evening
news, I decided to divert as many resources
as possible, and so called in a bomb threat to
the police. I told them there were hostages at
what remained of the old Crossroads

settlement and if they didn't bring every resource they had, I would detonate the bomb. I never thought it would work, but here I was. Stringing a dead woman's bowels around a sign like Christmas fairy lights, without a soul in sight. Such is the nosy and inquisitive nature of people in the 2020's that all of the residents around the sea front had ran to their cars or grabbed taxis to go and gawk at what was happening at Crossroads. I had never felt so free in my life.

Once I had finished my display, I stood back and admired my work. I was not sure if this was going to work, or if Player Two had left any evidence at all. Other than the indication of their skill in opening up my parents, I had not yet seen any. However, neither could I see any evidence left by myself. Then came the doubt about my own actions. Had I gone too far?

This had all started accidentally many years ago. I had allowed the bloodlust to develop to the levels it now had, and I was now in this situation because of my own actions. The thing that made me realise I was exactly where I wanted to be was as I watched the blood on the intestines catch the light as the sun began to descend, and I smiled. Of course I was where I wanted to be. I had purpose, and the game was not going to reach its conclusion until Player Two was behind bars, or worse.

When I returned to my apartment, I switched on the TV, and the news was reporting how the hoax at Crossroads was now being investigated along with an internal investigation over how every resource was diverted resulting in mild looting on Main Street.

I sat on the couch for a moment and contemplated the recent series of events. I also contemplated who would read these words one day. Who was I documenting all of this for? I had no children, no apprentices, nobody who knew what I was capable of, or had done. I did not even know who Player Two was. Nevertheless, I am glad I have expressed myself with accuracy and to the best of my ability. Maybe as I wait for what happens next, this journal will one day reach a point where I can write the words 'Game Over.'

THIRTEEN

I read those final words of Armand's journal, and my own mind wandered a little. He truly did have a love for his craft. Then again, he had never reached my own levels, despite him being considerably older, and with a much stranger upbringing than myself. I pitied him really. He had never reached his full potential. The ease with which I found him and discovered what he was doing was almost laughable. I gave him the chance to become my equal, but he never quite rose to the occasion.

The last straw for me, was his pathetic attempt to frame me by hanging those pig bowels all over the pier sign. I mean surely there must have been some level of doubt within him that they were not human. Perhaps he wanted to be caught. Perhaps he was secretly looking for a way out. Then again, his abandonment of his measured and planned methods happened far too quickly. I did not alter his life that much in such a short space of time. But now here we were.

The only thing I can say about him, is that he was a good fuck. Most of the *Jersey Shore* wannabes in this shithole of a town are just looking to get their dick away and have a self-indulgent conquest of a hot woman, and then move on bragging about it while the woman lies there nowhere near satisfaction, and contemplating if she actually felt anything at all.

Not Armand, though. He was inexperienced and enjoyed being led. The obsession he seemed to have for my nipple piercings made the whole thing even more enjoyable. He was always so tender in touching them, but I helped him to learn to be a little less reserved. Shame about his killing skills though. I wonder why we killers keep these journals. As Armand had asked, what is the actual point? Are we writing them for a future true crime documentary, or is it just for our own sadistic pleasure to one day look back and feel a sense of accomplishment?

Armand will never know.

He only came to about half an hour ago. I imagine the surprise of seeing my face probably sent him into shock, because he passed out again almost immediately. Then again, it could also be the blood loss. I did slice him pretty bad. Forgive me as I smile at that image. He doesn't only fuck good, he *tastes* good.

I placed his vial next to the others in my refrigerator. Dressing for my next salad. The main course was to come, however. As I walked back into the main part of the warehouse, to see his still hanging naked body dangling from the chains I had installed in the roof, I saw he had regained consciousness once more. Not bad. Only out for ten minutes this time. I guess I owed him an explanation before I completed the game.

I grabbed a nearby fold-up chair, carried it over to him, and sat directly in front of him. His eyes were panicked, and his breathing rapid.

"Hello lover," I said as seductively as possible.

"You fucking cunt."

He spat blood at my feet. A nice touch.

"It was all a setup?" he growled at me.

I found it very hard to prevent my smile.

"You obviously weren't as clever as you thought you were, Armand. I tracked you from the very first level."

He looked perplexed. The first level had of course been all the way back in his college days. But I was there. I was in the crowd watching my big brother graduate. I was a child who wandered off from the crowd only to witness Armand cause the redneck bully's death. I watched the blood drip down the pitchfork, and I saw Armand's face. That was when I knew, there would be more to come.

He listened to me retell my story, his eyes bulging ever wider, the blood now dried on his chest from the slash I gave him as I cut his clothes free. I continue, twisting and tearing at his mind and cutting through everything he thought he knew.

I told him in great detail about how Andrew felt inside of me. Armand had been so obsessed with his own goals, that he hadn't even recognised me. I was the girl he hired to seduce Andrew. I was the girl he had arrested. He framed me for Andrew's murder. Luckily the evidence was circumstantial, and I was released. It was then that I plotted my revenge. I would join this little game of his, and toy with him before I took the final victory.

"You really don't recognise me from that night do you?" I asked him.

There was nothing for a moment or two, and then I released he was now reliving the memory. And there it was.

"Your… your hair is different. Your clothes, your face. You look different."

I scoffed at him. Like nobody committing a murder had ever used plastic surgery before. The time between Armand completing level 2 and starting level 3 had left me with plenty of time to upgrade my appearance. Only slight modifications, of course. I knew my own beauty. A couple of shots of Botox, a lip filler here and there. Change your hairstyle and nobody recognises you. Not in this day and age.

Everyone is disposable to everyone else. Such is the world we now live in.

I decided I would join his game after Andrew. What I didn't decide was what happened next. In my brief stint in prison, I was jumped by a woman who considered herself to be the dominant one in the wing. The boss. The chief. Yeah right.

She decided I was going to be her bitch because of my looks being far superior to anyone else in the wing. I decided otherwise. I elbowed her in the face when she grabbed me from behind, and her nose exploded with blood all over my own face and some went into my mouth.

My instinct was to spit it out, but the taste…

Something about the taste of her warm blood trickling over my tongue brought… excitement! While she was flailing about, I rushed up to her and kissed her hard on the lips, absorbing as much of the sweet crimson as I could, before the guards split us up. They figured it was a lesbian romance gone wrong. Not much intelligence in the prison service.

I watched Armand's face morph into something I had seen plenty of times before. Horror. Pure horror. I detailed to him how I had eaten his mother's tongue with a fried egg the day after I killed her. I munched on his father's index finger after I threw it on the barbecue with some roasted peppers and honey for extra sweetness. Human flesh in a smoker is simply divine.

I had intended to feast on the mayor too, but time restraints prevented that. It had taken me longer than I expected to recover Armand's shoes from the sea, by which point I only had time to taste the son.

"That reminds me. I must remember to eat the rest of him before I restock that deep freeze."

Armand lost his composure at that point and he vomited all over his front and onto the floor in front of me. I was not impressed.

"Well we can't have that now, can we? Hardly sanitary."

I walked over to the near wall where a fire hose was mounted. Switching it on, I blasted a large stream of water at Armand, firing away any trace of vomit, along with the smell. The chair was blown away too, but that was of no matter. I had no intention of sitting down with my colleague again. When I turned off the hose, I realised the pressure had hurt him more than I had intended. His left wrist was now broken from where the force of the jet had hit him and he twisted in surprise. His screams were rather pathetic. Nothing like the screams of ecstasy we had shared. I leaned over my dinner table, and picked up the cleaver, dragging the tip of the blade against the wood as I did so.

There was something so seductive about a sharp blade. The kill always felt more personal when you could feel the vibrations in your own hand of the flesh and the muscle tearing apart. It was the same sensation I received when eating the flesh too. I shuddered with the memory of such a pleasurable experience.

"If it helps you to know, Armand, you were the best fuck I ever had."

"That's of great comfort," he retorted between gasps for breath.

He saw the glint of the knife, but his energy was gone. There was nowhere for him to go, and he finally understood that I was going to be the one to complete the game first.

"And as such, I wanted a memento of the special times we shared."

I couldn't help but sport a wide grin as I swung the blade of the knife downwards. His screams echoed around the warehouse, but it had long been abandoned by the previous occupants. Some experimental medical facility had been driven out of here, and not long after, I moved in. It was the ideal home for my culinary tastes.

It took quite a while for Armand to bleed to death. I always leave my meat hanging, it enhances the flavour. I washed off the knife in the sink on the far wall, before returning to the body with my tweezers and a freezer bag. As I placed Armand's manhood into the bag, and sealed the ziplock bag, I smiled again. This would not be food, this would be a trophy. I had a special draw for that.

I would soon have to move from this place however. Rumblings were apparent that the previous occupants were trying to start up their business again, and I suspected before long I'd be driven out, so felt it would be better to leave of my own accord.

I placed the bag in the special draw where I kept my most prized possessions. My first boyfriend had a wonderful tattoo on his hip that I couldn't bear to throw away, and so I placed Armand's bag next to the flat piece of skin and shut the draw.

I opened the journal that had been a fascinating read, and as I scribbled on the bottom of Armand's last entry, I had to giggle to myself.

'Player 1 : GAME OVER'

I shut the book, and pushed it to one side. In front of me was my own journal, much thicker than Armand's had been. I pulled it close to me, and opened the book to the most recent page. I wrote my newest entry.

'Level 64 complete. Level 65 begins.'

AFTERWORD

Well I do hope you have managed to contain some of your lunch, or whatever meal you recently ate. I understand that was a bit of a wild ride towards the end.

If I hadn't already made it clear with Frame of Mind, that my books were stalking into darker territory, then I hope I have with this one. Although short at around 100 pages, this is in my opinion, a compacted novel rather than a story written to be short. I could have easily fleshed this out into a full length novel in the Dark Corner Universe, but I also wanted to make it a true one-off.

We will never visit the character of Jenny, or hear mention of Armand and his game in the main series. Could there be another novella regarding these characters? No.

Sorry for the tease, but the whole point of this new breed of novellas, is that they are quick to produce, and are kept isolated on their own. I'm not looking to do a secondary spin-off series through this medium.

I do hope that the story was enjoyable to fans of my existing work, and also any newcomers to the series. If you were intrigued by my tale of murder, deception and blood, then I have many more for you to read. You can find details of all of those books and places to find them at the end of this afterword.

What I can tell you, is that the next book will return to the main series and will be the fantasy horror adventure, The Land Beyond.

The horror element is a recent addition to TLB, due to the events of Frame of Mind being previously unscheduled, and while it will not be dominant in TLB, the darker horror elements will be present in all my works going forward so keep an eye out for any new developments and announcements.

Once again, thank you for joining me on this journey, and I hope to see you sat in the Dark Corner once again in the very near future.

Dave.

ABOUT THE AUTHOR

David William Adams, born in 1988, is a predominantly horror focussed author from Wolverhampton, United Kingdom. He attended the prestigious Thomas Telford School located in Telford, Shropshire until he decided during the first year of sixth form, that his studies were not taking him in the direction he wanted to go. At that point, he left higher education and entered retail work.

In 2007, David and his family relocated to Ilfracombe, North Devon, to start a fresh life following the death of David's grandfather. He worked for local greengrocer Norman's Fruit & Veg for 8 years.

In 2014, he met Charlotte, and following her move to Plymouth to pursue university studies, in 2016, David also relocated to join her.

In 2018, he and Charlotte were married.

During the Coronavirus pandemic in 2020, David lost his retail job, and restarted his writing work, having never previously been published as an adult. In January 2021, whilst working for a courier company, David published his first collection of short horror stories, The Dark Corner.

In March 2021, he published the sequel anthology, Return to the Dark Corner, and in July 2021 he published his first novel, Wealdstone, which was set in the same universe as the first two books and featured the teaming up of the recurring characters.

In December 2021, David published his first science fiction novel, Resurrection, but found himself missing the characters from the earlier books.

However, in 2022, David and Charlotte welcomed their first child, Molly and so writing was put on the back burner for a year, until in 2023 he published the sequel to Wealdstone, entitled Wealdstone : Crossroads.

Early in 2023, all of David's published books were brought under the umbrella of the Dark Corner Literary Universe across all social media.

June 2023 saw the release of the darkest instalment in the series so far, Frame of Mind and with 2 more releases due for 2023, David shows no signs of slowing down.

CONNECTING WITH THE AUTHOR

You can find all of my social media pages using the same handle below. I also do four livestreams per week on my TikTok page where you can ask me about my books, the series, where it's going, and hear any new developments first hand. You can also buy my books in the same streams.

THE DARK CORNER LITERARY UNIVERSE

This series began as a short horror story compilation in 2020, with its roots as far back as 2001 when I had the idea for a story called 'The Medallion.' That story stayed with me for over a decade, along with another one I titled 'Dead Miner Walking' but never finished.

Eventually those two stories sere blended together and then separated to create the very first story in the original Dark Corner book called 'The White Dress.' Elements of the Medallion story would then feature in three stories linked together across the first two books.

Originally, I had not intended to make each of the short stories in the same universe, but as I did so, I saw interesting plot points arise and I wanted to see how much of a universe I could actually create here. This led to the first novel in the series, Wealdstone, which had several of the characters from the short stories in the first 2 books, team up to take on a big bad.

Once I had completed that novel, I decided to try my hand at another passion of mine, science fiction. From there, I wrote Resurrection. It was a tale set in the future where Earth is destroyed in an unprovoked and unexpected attack, but one woman is saved by an alien captain. The story then follows her as she tries to track down a piece of technology that can bring humanity back from the dead.

Originally, Resurrection was not going to be part of the Dark Corner Universe, until when re-reading it for a new edition, I noticed that the main character, Molly, had stated her hometown was Wealdstone. It made me chuckle when I realised I was still writing Dark Corner books even though they weren't horror.

It was at this point that I decided to actively brand the entire series so far as The Dark Corner Literary Universe.

After the publication of Resurrection, people were asking me if there would be a sequel to Wealdstone, and if I was done with horror, and I reassured them that I had every intention of carrying on that part of the series, but following the birth of our first baby in February 2022, I decided to take a year off.

And then in March of 2023, Wealdstone : Crossroads was published, to a very good reception. It was the most successful book to date and sold more copies than any other in the series, and continues to do so even now. Following my launch on TikTok and setting up a shop there to sell my books and directly interact with my readers, a small group of those readers who have now become dear friends, suggested that September was too long to wait for the next instalment, and so with my publishing restrictions lifted by KDP, I was able to do what I wanted for the first time in 2 years.

Over the next 6 weeks, I conjured the idea, wrote and published the sixth book in the series, Frame of Mind on 12th June 2023. This was by far and away the darkest and most violent and disturbing book I had written so far, but again it was received with astounding praise and is quickly approaching the sales figures of Wealdstone : Crossroads. With the seventh book in the series due for release in September 2023, The Land Beyond,

I found myself getting restless as having to go so long without writing anything new. One of my newfound friends, Iona, as mentioned in the foreword, suggested an unattached novella. Just something I could write and publish quickly to get a story idea out of my system, but so there was something to read between FOM and TLB.

And that is where this book came from. The Game is the first novella in the Dark Corner Universe, and is completely unattached to the rest of the series other than its setting. There are no recurring characters, no strong references to the other books, and is officially a completely stand alone title, meaning you can read it at any time.

The plan is to scatter these novellas throughout the series in each phase going forward, as The Land Beyond will be followed by the third Wealdstone novel, currently branded with the working title of Wealdstone : Origins (likely to change before release) to close the first phase of these stories.

While the next novella may be a year away, I can promise there will indeed be more, and if this is the branch which snags you as you walk by and grabs your attention to enter the rest of this universe, then I would be ecstatic.

I hope to keep your attention for many years to come, and in case you haven't worked it out yet, here is the publishing order for the books in the main series so far.

- The Dark Corner
- Return to the Dark Corner
- Wealdstone
- Resurrection
- Wealdstone : Crossroads
- Frame of Mind

THE GAME – A DARK CORNER NOVELLA

Are you seeking support for your mental health, distress, or trauma?

Look no further! Flare Peer Support is here for you. We may not be professional counsellors, but we are a compassionate peer support group that believes in the power of connection and understanding.

Talk it Out Thursdays: Every Thursday, we host structured and activity-based sessions where you can share your thoughts and experiences in a safe and supportive environment.

Self-Care Sundays: Our relaxed Sundays are dedicated to practising self-care, having fun, and building a strong community. Join us as we create a nurturing space for relaxation and rejuvenation.

We understand that some individuals may require more personalised and regular support. That's why we offer one-to-one sessions for those who feel the need for a deeper connection.

Feeling the need for a trusted confidant? Our Key-Mentor Programme pairs you with a supportive mentor who will check up on you semi-regularly. Your mentor will be there to listen, offer guidance, and provide a private space for you to express your concerns, issues, or problems happening in your life.

You don't have to face your struggles alone. Join Flare today and become a part of a caring community that understands and supports you on your journey toward mental well-being.

Find out more about Flare at
ALLMYLINKS.COM/FLARECARES

Printed in Great Britain
by Amazon

23912542R00072